The Martian Tales

MARILEE ROBIN BURTON
ILLUSTRATED BY KRISTIN BARR

Rigby

Contents

Prologue

Sanders A. Parker was a quirky kid. His hair was curly red. He always wore something in his favorite color—purple. He buttoned his shirts from the bottom up. He read how-to books and stories about wild animals, strange insects, and the histories of things like bathtubs or buttons. He put his left shoe on first on Mondays, Wednesdays, and Fridays. He started with the right shoe on Tuesdays, Thursdays, and Saturdays. Sunday was a free-choice day.

But quirkiest of all was the fact that Sanders came from Mars. This was something he'd only recently realized. And now that he knew it, he didn't want anyone else to know. Not his mother, not his father, not even his best friend, Joey Ferarro.

Sanders understood that his reason for being on Earth had to be kept secret. He, Sanders A. Parker, had been sent to report on certain aspects of life on the planet. Certain sad aspects of Earth life that happened, through no fault of their own, to kids. Or in particular, *one* certain sad aspect of Earth life that happened through no fault of his own, to *one* kid. To Sanders A. Parker.

Or was it? wondered Sanders about the no-fault part. And if it *was* his fault, how could he fix it? Even if it wasn't, how could he fix it? Because he wanted to fix it. He wanted to solve the problem, change the situation, find the solution. *That* was his secret assignment: to report on the whole thing—problem, situation, solution. He was going to write about it all in an intergalactic planetary journal. *That* was his secret mission.

Sanders came to realize all this on the last day of school. Up until then, he had been a regular (if there is such a thing) Earth kid. The day began almost like any other, except that it was the last day of school. Sanders never suspected anything. Oh, maybe deep down inside he might have had an inkling. But way up top he was just too excited about school ending and summer beginning to think about or notice any other kind of beginning or ending.

1

The Beginning
of the End

"Sanders, are you up yet?" his mother asked, knocking gently on his door first thing that morning.

Yes, he was. Awake anyway, if not up. Far-off car horns mixing with close-up cat purrs had woken him earlier. But he still lay in bed, imagining the day to come. The pizza party, the summer songs and poems, the happy good-byes. And then he and Joey would walk home. School over, summer just beginning. That's where Sanders' imaginings led him. Joey and him with a whole summer and no plans at all. Well, some plans, actually. The best kinds—his and Joey's.

Sanders looked up at the sparkly stars he and Joey had pasted on his ceiling one night. I wonder who invented pizza? he thought.

"Sanders, are you up yet?"

"Yes. Yes. Yes," he answered. And by the third yes, he really was. He washed. He dressed. He put on clean jeans, his favorite purple shirt, black socks, black sneakers, and a cap with a hound dog logo.

Ready for the day, Sanders bounded downstairs. He started out one step at a time, then two, then three. He hadn't yet been able to make a four-step leap. Soon. Maybe before summer ended. But for now, he took the steps one, two, three at a time. Then three, two, and one.

"Hey, Dad!"

"Morning, Sanders." His father looked up from the business news, tired eyes and bushy eyebrows peeping over the paper. "Sleep OK?"

"Pretty good, I guess," Sanders said, grabbing the box of Toasty Oats cereal. "Only the night seemed really long. I couldn't wait for the day to begin. It's the end!"

"Yes, some nights can seem longer than others," his dad agreed.

Sanders poured cereal into his bowl, still thinking about the day ahead. "Do we have any bananas?" he asked.

"Yes, sweetie," his mother assured him. "You know we always have bananas." But she didn't get up to get him one. And she didn't comment even though Sanders could see she, too, must be thinking about his last day. Instead, she sat stirring the cream into her coffee for an extra long time.

Sanders got up to get a banana.

"Bring me one, too, will you?" his father requested.

"Sure," Sanders said. "How about trading a banana for the funnies?"

"Sounds like a good deal," his father answered as he riffled through the stack of papers next to him. "Here you go," he said, handing Sanders the local news.

Before opening the section to expose the full page of comics hidden within, Sanders glanced at the front page. "Big change ahead," the lead headline said. But Sanders didn't have time to read the article. He didn't even want to read it. He was anxious to see what was fun or funny inside and then rush off to meet Joey.

He folded the paper to the comics and set it on the table beside his cereal bowl. He sliced bananas into his cereal and added milk. On his left, his father was still scouring the business section. On his right, his mother was leafing through the weekend calendar. Sanders dove into the day's funnies.

Breakfast was especially quiet that morning. But Sanders didn't think much about that. His mind was filled with noisy thoughts about the day ahead. And other than the quiet, everything was starting just as it always did.

Mostly.

2

The Last Day

It took Sanders and Joey 13 minutes and 27 seconds to walk to school that day. That was the shared part of the trip. They always met in the middle, in the empty lot halfway between their two houses. They never counted the alone part. They timed the walk from the exact middle of the lot to the first step at the door of the school.

Timing the walk to school was an ongoing experiment. Today, Sanders had guessed it would take 14 minutes and 11 seconds. Joey thought it would be 12 minutes and 53 seconds. The truth lay in between the two. That's why the boys were such good partners. They always met in the middle.

"Do you think peanut-butter pizza would be a good invention?" Sanders asked as they climbed up the steps. He thought they might add it to their list of things to make or do or invent during the summer.

"Not with tomato sauce," Joey said with a frown.

"No, you'd have to use a different kind of sauce," Sanders agreed. "Maybe apple?"

"I don't think so," Joey said, opening the classroom door.

Sanders and Joey had been working together most of the school year. Researching, exploring, experimenting—and becoming friends. It had started when Mrs. Ryan asked them to be Space Partners. The "Two Potatoes" they had called themselves when she'd asked them to do a report on the planet Mars. They picked the name because of Phobos and Deimos, the two potato-shaped Mars moons. Joey was the potato fan. He liked them mashed, baked, or French-fried.

Later, though, they changed their name to the "Mars Partners" because it seemed more scientific. The name stuck even when the Exploration of Space unit ended. They liked to joke that their friendship had started on Mars.

Sanders hadn't really expected to become best friends with Joey. They were different—at least he thought so. After all, he was a quiet, keep-to-himself kind of kid. Joey was noisy and all over the place. But they'd ended up being friends, just the same. Good friends. They always met in the middle.

There were three different kinds of pizza at the class party that afternoon. Peanut-butter pizza was not one of them.

"Someone should invent it," Sanders told Joey. Sanders was fond of peanut butter, especially the chunky kind.

"Peanut butter is OK," said Joey, "but I'm not sure about putting it on pizza. At least, I don't think that would be considered much of an invention. How about inventing flying skates?" he suggested. "Or a meteor net? Or a rock-making machine?"

"But you're underestimating the value of peanut butter," Sanders laughed.

"Well, we have more important plans for the summer than making peanut-butter pizza," Joey responded.

"Yeah, but it could be one of the things we work on," Sanders suggested. He stood on a chair to take down the papier-mâché model of the solar system he and Joey had created earlier in the year. "It's probably the perfect food to take into orbit," he added.

The peanut-butter discussion ended when Mrs. Ryan called the class together for a good-bye speech. In front of her was a cardboard box full of gifts that looked suspiciously booklike.

"This has been a great year," Mrs. Ryan told the class. "We've learned a lot together. But learning doesn't stop when summer begins." She reached into the box and pulled out one of the packages.

"I'm sure each one of you will continue to learn many things over the summer," she continued. "I hope that you'll all write about your summer explorations and observations."

Mrs. Ryan handed Sanders the first package. It had a purple card taped on top.

Well, maybe, Sanders thought when he tore off the wrapping paper and found a journal inside. It might be fun to write about the things he and Joey did together this summer.

"Remember, good-bye is just a beginning," Mrs. Ryan told her students as they walked out the door that day.

3

A Lucky Rock

"Sixteen minutes, 8 seconds," Sanders said, looking at his watch. That's how long it had taken them to get to the middle of the empty lot on the way home. The same distance had taken longer than it had in the morning because Sanders had walked backward. "So I can look back on the year," he'd told Joey. Of course, walking backward had also made him trip on a rock that he hadn't been able to see.

Joey had thought it wiser to walk frontward. "So I can see summer coming," he'd said. He may not have been the first one to see summer, but he did see the rock. Of course, Joey probably would have seen the rock first even if Sanders hadn't been walking backward. After all, he'd been collecting rocks since age five and had an eagle eye for interesting new specimens.

As Sanders picked himself up off the dusty ground, Joey bent down and picked up the rock. "Looks lucky," he said.

"Lucky for who?" Sanders asked. "I tripped over it!"

"Lucky for us!" Joey said. "Look at the color. It's red.

Like a Martian rock. It must mean it's going to be a good summer for the Mars Partners."

"We already know that!" Sanders exclaimed.

Joey nodded. "Well, now it's for sure!" he said, slipping the rock in his pocket. "A rock from *our* planet."

"Yeah," Sanders agreed without having really examined the rock.

"Or it might be gneiss or a breccia rock," Joey said. "Or granite. I guess I'll have to test it to know if it's from Earth or Mars!"

The boys said good-bye and headed off in opposite directions, each walking facing forward. A few minutes later Sanders was standing on his doorstep. He rummaged through his pocket, then pulled out the front door key.

The key was new—bright and shiny with handsome jagged edges. He carried it on a ring that also sported a purple glowdog and a compass. If you put the glowdog under a light for 30 seconds and then turned the light off, the dog would glow. Not an exceptionally useful object, but Sanders liked it.

The compass was true. Its needle pointed north whichever way Sanders turned. "So you can always find your way home," his dad once told him.

Now Sanders put the key in the lock and jiggled it. Click.

"Smooth as butter!" Sanders said to himself—the exact words his father had used when they fixed the old lock.

"Good job, Sandy," Dad had said next, even though he was the one who really did all the work fixing it. Sanders thought his father could fix almost anything. He wanted that skill, too. It would help when his inventions went awry.

Sanders pushed the door open and took his first step into what was now officially summer vacation.

"Anybody home?" he called. And then, "Whoops!" He had bumped into a box of clothing that stood in the middle of the entry hall.

"Huh?" Sanders straightened his glasses to make sure he was seeing correctly. Usually his mom warned him ahead of time when she gathered stuff to donate to the local homeless shelter. "I'm not putting any of my stuff in these boxes," he announced to the empty room. "I need my old clothes for summer sleuthing."

"Anybody home?" he called again as he headed into the kitchen. "No one here, either?" he queried the cat who lazed on a chair. Then he apologized, "Sorry, Maxie. You're someone, I know."

Sanders climbed up on the chair next to Maxie's. He looped the string of the papier-mâché model from the light fixture so the solar system dangled above the kitchen table. He was especially proud of how he and Joey had made sure Mars had her two potato moons. "Fear" and "panic" was what the words *Phobos* and *Deimos* meant.

Looking past the two small moons, Sanders could see

through the kitchen window and out into the backyard. His parents were both home. They were sitting across from each other at the patio table and talking. It looked serious. The last day of school was a half day and his dad was already home. Sanders wondered what was going on.

He jumped down, leaving the dangling solar system behind with the sleeping cat, and went out to explore parent territory.

"Hi! What's up?" Sanders asked.

Not for a moment did he expect that his world would soon tilt and go off-kilter just like the planet Uranus in its orbit. No, he never expected it.

Oh, they could have told him they were moving to Alaska or Australia or Timbuktu. Or that they were going to raise okapis in the backyard. Or bats in the belfry. Or maybe that his father was going to build a belfry (with Sanders' help, even).

Nothing would have surprised him more than what they *did* say. "What do you mean?" he asked, his heart sinking to his feet.

"Your mother and I have been having some trouble lately. We haven't been getting along the way we used to. We each need some time alone. We're going to separate for a little while."

Sanders wasn't sure what "not getting along the way we used to" meant. But "separate" he knew. It wasn't good. Leah Marshall's parents had separated last year. And it wasn't just for a little while. Now Leah had two houses and two sets of parents. She was always moving back and forth between them. At school she told everyone how great it was to have double everything. But you sure couldn't tell how great it was from looking at her. She seemed sad all the time. And right after it happened, just when she was first bragging about having two of everything, Sanders had spied her crying during study hall time.

"Separate" was not a good thing.

"Why?" he asked.

But they didn't really answer that question. Instead they explained that they both loved him. Loved him very much. And that this didn't change that at all. That he would still have a mother and a father. That he would still be the most important thing in both their lives. Just that they wouldn't all be together at the same time.

He knew what he wanted to say—what he would have liked to say—what he even thought he tried to say: "Can't you talk it out? You always tell me to talk it out when I have a problem. Isn't 'trouble' a problem?"

But he didn't say it. The thoughts didn't come as fast as the feelings and the only words that came out were "No! You can't! You can't! You can't! You can't!"

At least that's how Sanders remembered it later. Maybe he did say something else. Maybe he did ask questions. Maybe he did explain to them why he didn't think it was a good idea. Or what would be a better idea. But he hadn't found exactly the right words. Because he was sure that if he could have found just the right words to explain why they really *couldn't* separate—then they really *wouldn't*.

Only . . . they were going to do it. And his most important question was still unanswered.

What would happen to *him?*

4

Intergalactic Investigating

The conversation with his parents lasted either a short time or a long one—Sanders wasn't sure which. Afterward, he went up to his room, climbing the steps one by one by one.

His heart was racing, or it had stopped. He didn't know which there, either. Inside he was jagged and zigzagged like the edges of the new front door key. "I need to go to my office," he said aloud.

Sanders tossed his backpack on his bed and pulled the old camping tent out from underneath. It was rolled tight inside the box because he hadn't used it recently. He hadn't needed alone time in a while.

He dumped the tent out on the floor, unrolling the fabric to retrieve the bag of support rods. He put three short pieces together to make one long, flexible rod. Then he put three more pieces together to make a second rod. He slipped the ends of the two rods into the pockets at the edge of the tent base, forming a skeleton around the outside. Like a crab skeleton sits outside a crab, he thought.

The skeleton gave form and shape to the dome—a private office in the middle of the bedroom. Sanders grabbed his backpack and took it inside.

"All alone," he said with a sigh. He unzipped the backpack and took out Mrs. Ryan's gift. He read the card she'd attached.

Every good-bye has a hello in it. Find it.
Fondly,
Mrs. Ryan

Sanders crumpled the card and stuffed it in the bottom of his backpack. He opened the summer journal and started to write.

MARS JOURNAL NUMBER 1
Earth Date: June 22, 1:43:11 P.M.

My name is Sanders A. Parker and I'm from outer space. I know that now. I was born on Mars and brought to Earth in an invisible rocket ship long before my eleventh birthday. I must have been secretly placed (secret from my parents) in the Parker house.

This is where my career as an intergalactic investigative reporter is to begin. My job is to write and report for the news journals of the invisible people of the planet Mars. Also for the other planetary systems in cooperation with the Solar League.

Of course, my parents have no knowledge of this. Their memories were implanted with the belief that I am their true child. They believe I was born to them by natural means, a natural Earth child. It is better all around that they continue to think this and not know the true details of my outer space origin. Of course, on occasion, I believe my Earth mother may have suspected the truth. For example, on days when I forget to make my bed or put yesterday's dirty socks in the laundry, she seems startled. She comes into my room, takes a look around, and says, "Sanders, it looks like you're from outer space." Does she know the truth?

But to be honest with you, I didn't even remember I was an extraterrestrial until today. When I came home from school, my parents told me they weren't getting along like they used to. They told me they were having trouble. They told me they were separating. That's when I remembered.

Maybe the Martians had seen it coming and wanted to get the inside scoop on parent trouble from a kid's point of view. So maybe that's why they sent me here to begin with. I wonder what my Martian parents are like? For sure, they still get along just like they used to. For sure, they will always get along just like they used to. And they will never need to separate. This I'm absolutely sure of. Parents on Mars don't separate. Parents on Mars stay together.

Now, let me tell you about snails. Did you know snails are also from the planet Mars? Yes, it's true. I didn't bring them all with me when I came. No. Martians have been secretly depositing snails on Earth for thousands of years. It's because their antennas are very useful to Martians, passing along outer space radio waves and helping alien creatures communicate with one another on a foreign planet.

Sanders clicked his pen so the nib with the purple ink retreated like a turtle into its shell. He closed the journal and put it back in his backpack. Then he went downstairs to find and relocate some snails.

5

Snails

Joey was already there waiting when Sanders got to the empty lot, a large brown sack full of snails in his hand.

"How many?" Joey asked.

"Thirty-seven," Sanders answered, looking away from Joey so his friend wouldn't notice that he had been crying. Inside the bag were 37 snails. It hadn't taken him long to collect them.

Snail relocation was an idea that had come from Sanders' mother. "I'm a snail pacifist," she had explained to Sanders and Joey. She didn't want to poison the snails but didn't want them eating her geraniums, either. So she paid a nickel a snail to relocate them to some other place. A place where they could lead as happy a life as they had been leading under the geraniums. Or maybe not quite as happy a life, but at least a healthy one. That was the snail relocation plan.

Sometimes Joey helped Sanders search for snails. It could be an interesting occupation. But today Sanders had done it by himself. Today he had needed just a little bit more time alone to adjust to the tilt his world had taken.

So now, snails in hand, he was ready to face his friend. And he found that doing so gave him some reassurance that he hadn't completely fallen off the planet. But he didn't mention anything about that to Joey. He didn't want to discuss it or to tell Joey that he now knew that snails were intergalactic aliens. Or that he was a Martian.

Besides, reasoned Sanders, how would he explain what had happened at home? He didn't really understand it himself. Plus, he didn't want to say anything out loud about it because that would just make it more real. So he just asked, "Which bush do you think we should put the snails under?"

Joey found a good one—actually several good ones. They didn't want to put all 37 snails in one place, under one bush. That would cause overpopulation. Instead, they put 33 snails under five bushes, neatly dividing them up into little groups of friends. (If snails had friends.) They reserved four snails to take to Joey's house for scientific investigation. Not unkind investigation—they were snail pacifists, too. They would simply study them so they could learn and explore, as Mrs. Ryan had always encouraged them to do. Then they would relocate them.

"You can take the snails to my room," Joey said when they reached his house. "I'll go see if I can find a plastic container to keep them in."

"Don't forget to get some lettuce, too," Sanders reminded his friend. He walked into Joey's room to wait. It was a mess—as always. Backpack and books spread out all over the bed. Shoes and magazines on the floor. Maps, markers, a magnifying glass, egg cartons filled with rocks, and just plain rocks all over the desk. Sanders didn't think Joey ever put anything away. How could he find anything? Sanders' mom would never let him get away with this, though he wished she would. He hated cleaning up.

Sanders pushed Joey's backpack aside to make a place to sit.

There was the red rock—the one they found on the way home from school. The one Joey claimed after Sanders tripped over it walking backward. The one Joey said looked like it was from planet Mars. The one he said was lucky.

"A lucky rock from the planet Mars," Sanders said to himself. He picked it up to study it more closely. It was a pretty rock. It fit right in his hand. He could close his fist around it comfortably. It had a smooth place on one side and a rough place on the other. It would fit in any number of pockets. It made him feel good to hold the Martian rock. Like it belonged there in his hand.

Sanders knew that it was really just a plain old rock—and that it was Joey's. He knew that in his head. But still, when he heard his friend's footsteps coming down the hall, it was as if his head forgot to tell his hands what to do. He stuffed the rock into his side pocket before he could think about it more.

"How's this for a guest house for snails?" Joey asked, holding up a large clear container.

"Good," Sanders said. "Just right."

6

The Plan

Sanders held Joey's rock in his left hand all the way home. He wasn't exactly sure why he'd taken it. He knew he shouldn't have, that it wasn't right to take things without asking—even a rock. It felt especially bad to be sneaking something from a friend.

Sanders counted footsteps from Joey's house to his own. Eight hundred and forty-three. He wondered if the number would have been the same if he'd walked backward. He knew it would be close. But would it be the same? He wondered what to do about the rock. *He wondered what to do about his parents!* He knew they would still be his parents even if they weren't together. But would *that* be the same? Sanders didn't think so. "Eight hundred and forty-four," he said out loud. That was the step up to the door.

"Sanders, you home? Come on in here with us, will you?" his father called from the living room.

His parents were sitting there talking. They were sure talking a lot for two people who wanted time away from each other. Sanders slumped down into the easy chair across from them, straightening his glasses so he could see clearly.

"Sandy, I just got off the phone with Grandpa," his mother said.

"Is he OK?" Sanders asked. He hadn't seen his grandfather since the summer before. That was when the whole family had traveled across the country for his grandmother's funeral. He'd been close to Gram. At least, closer to her than to his grandfather. She was the one who always called on his birthday and holidays and even days that weren't special at all. She was the one who had always remembered what he'd told her the last time they had spoken. She was the one he'd spent time with when they visited. His grandfather was always busy working. Sanders didn't really even know his grandfather at all.

"Oh yes, dear, he's fine. Dad is just fine. In fact, he'd like you to come and stay with him for the summer."

"What?" Sanders asked, crinkling his forehead as if that would make him hear better—or understand better. Why would his grandfather want him to come and visit? Especially now. They'd never been close. And why for the whole summer? His grandmother wasn't even there anymore. And right now Sanders needed to stay close to home. There was an important reason for that. He had a mission, after all.

"Isn't that a wonderful idea?" his mother was saying. "You can go to Shady Point until school starts."

"No!" Sanders exclaimed. "It's *not* a good idea. It's not a good idea at all." Why were his parents sending him away? And how could they think it was a good idea?

"Sanders, think about it," said his father. "Summer at your grandpa's would be fun. You could hike and hunt frogs and climb trees. You could spend some time getting to know him better."

"I don't want to go," Sanders said, his hand tightening around Joey's rock. He didn't want to get to know his grandpa better. He didn't want to leave home. He had plans with Joey. And most importantly, how could he get his parents to change their minds about separating if he wasn't here with them?

"It would be good for Grandpa, too," his mother added. "He's been lonely since Gram died."

"But I already have plans for the summer," Sanders said, his voice cracking.

His father stood up and walked over to him. "Sandy," he said, "things change. Plans change. We can't always do what we want to do. You'll understand better when you're older." He put one hand on Sanders' shoulder. "Your mother and I think it would be good for you to spend the summer with Grandpa. It will give us time to sort things out here. And you won't have to be in the middle of it."

"But I could help," Sanders said.

"No, Sanders. I'm not going to be here that much anyway. I've accepted a transfer to the Devonshire office for the summer. So I'm going to be spending a lot of my time there."

"Then I should stay here and help you, Mom."

"No, you can't," his mother said. "What with finishing up my nursing degree and working extra hours at the hospital now, I'm not going to be home much, either. The real help I need from you is to know you're safe and taken care of and having a good time."

"I can take care of myself," Sanders protested. He tried to use a responsible voice to impress them. "I don't have to go away."

"Honey, this isn't going to be easy for any of us," his mother said. "But I know you'll have a good time. There's so much for you to do in the country. And Grandpa will like having the company. It'll be good for both of you. It will be an adventure."

Sanders didn't agree. However, the words weren't there to explain to his parents the importance of his spending the summer at home in San Diego, California, rather than in Shady Point, Maine. How could he convince them to stay together, to be a family, if they sent him to the other end of the country?

And then there were all his plans with Joey, which suddenly seemed to take on more importance than they had moments before when he was still counting up to 843. How many steps away from Joey would he be in Shady Point? Or from his mother? Or father? A billion? And how

many miles would that make—48,546,000? That was the distance between Earth and Mars when the two planets were aligned in their orbits. And when they weren't . . . How many miles then?

Sanders' hand tightened around the rock. He couldn't give it back to Joey. Not right now.

MARS JOURNAL NUMBER 2
Earth Date: June 22, 4:57:18 P.M.

Adults on Earth don't remember what it's like to be a kid. It's like they walk through some big door when they grow up and leave everything they knew as a kid behind. Like they pack it all up in some suitcase and think they're going to take it with them. But when they get to that door, they're so excited about being a grown-up that they race through and leave the suitcase behind. Then once they're on the other side, they don't even remember that they even had this suitcase they were going to bring with them. Or what was in it. They don't remember they had it or packed it or anything. They even forget what the words mean—kid words, kid language. They speak a different language. And adults don't understand kid talk anymore.

So even though I was telling my Earth parents about why my summer plans were important, about why they should stay together, about why I needed to be with Joey . . . Even though I was saying all these words and explaining things clearly, they didn't understand. Because they didn't speak my language anymore. They don't understand what it means to be a kid. Martians understand. Parents don't. Not on Earth, at least.

MARS JOURNAL NUMBER 3
Earth Date: June 23, 7:13:22 A.M.

The weather and terrain on Mars are violent and varied. There are craters and canyons. There are gullies and volcanoes. The mountains are higher than the highest Earth mountains. The canyons are deeper than the deepest Earth canyons. There are strong winds and huge dust storms.

Sometimes it can be hard to come from such a planet. Sometimes, for a Martian, it feels like everything is trouble. Like parents who say they're having troubles. Sometimes Martian kids feel like they have troubles. Because look at what their planet is like. Sometimes it feels like trouble just to be a Martian.

7
Good-byes

He'd had almost a week before leaving for Maine. It wasn't enough. Only a few days to say good-bye to Joey. Good-bye to his dad. His mom would be a longer good-bye because she was taking him to Grandpa's. But even that good-bye wasn't going to be long enough.

Or maybe no amount of time would be long enough because he didn't want to say good-bye. He didn't want to go. After he first heard the news, he hadn't talked about it much to his parents, or even to Joey.

"Rough deal," Joey had said. He was disappointed, too, that they wouldn't be spending the summer together. Sanders still hadn't told him much about the separation. Not really. And he didn't tell Joey about Mars at all, or about the rock he had taken.

Now Sanders sat inside his tent office looking at the map. He traced his father's relocation route with his finger. He traced the road he and his mother would be driving from the Bangor airport to his grandfather's house in Shady Point. Both routes were highlighted—one in red and the other in blue. Neither one was marked in purple.

And there was a big gap of unhighlighted, unconnected space between the two.

His father had asked him to make sure the tent was down before he left. Outside the tent lay his canvas duffel bag, packed and waiting. He reviewed a mental list of the contents: T-shirts, jeans, socks, and underwear. His toothbrush. An atlas of spiders. Three other books—*Red Planet Research, A Short History of the Peanut,* and *Amazing Dog Stories.* Purple pens. His backpack. The Mars rock wasn't packed. He would carry it in his pocket.

It was almost time. "I don't want to go," he'd told his father that morning, really meaning "I don't want you to leave."

"I love you," his father had replied. Dad would be driving south to Devonshire at the exact same time that Sanders and his mother would be flying east to Maine. They would be going in different directions. Sanders took out his compass and studied it.

True north. No one was going true north. "You can always find your way home," his father had said. How? Sanders wondered.

"I don't want to go," Sanders had told his mother.

"We've been all through this, Sandy," she'd replied. "This is the best plan your father and I have been able to come up with. And you'll have a good time at Grandpa's. I know you will."

How did *she* know?

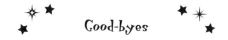

The cat nudged through the tent door to sneak into Sanders' private office. "I don't want to go, Maxie," he said, reaching down to stroke her soft fur. She began to purr. "But no one listens to me," he complained. "You're lucky. They aren't sending you away." Sanders unzipped his backpack and pulled out the summer journal.

MARS JOURNAL NUMBER 4
Earth Date: June 29, 9:05:10 A.M.

On Mars, kids can decide what they're going to do for the summer. Everybody on Mars knows kids make the best plans and the best decisions. On Earth, things are different, and parents are allowed to make all the decisions without ever asking kids what they think about it or what they really want to do. That would never happen on Mars.

Why didn't they ask me what I want to do? Why do they get to make all the decisions? Why don't I get to do what I want? Why can't I stay here with Joey?

Let me tell you what it's like on the planet Mars. Kids get to make all the decisions. I mean, ALL the decisions. Because kids are smarter than grown-ups. And on Mars, everybody knows that. So no decisions are made without first asking kids what they think about it. Kid conferences. They have kid conferences on Mars to see what kids think.

Also, Martian kids talk things over with their cats.

And cats give good advice. More people should listen to cats. On Mars, cats can talk. So can dogs. Most animals on Mars talk. Maybe the snails don't talk. But the snails have radio antennas. Cats' whiskers send out radio waves, too. A little. But cats are especially valuable at giving advice. They help kids decide what to do for the summer.

On Mars, if parents need time alone they go for a walk. They don't send kids away for the whole summer. To tell you the truth, I would really like to go back to Mars where I belong. Where parents don't send kids away. I don't want to go to Maine. I want to go where I belong—to Mars.

8

A Martian in Maine

It was afternoon when Sanders and his mother drove into Shady Point. They'd stayed in Bangor overnight and left there early in the morning for the long drive north. The busyness of buildings clumped one upon another faded away as cityscape was replaced by rolling hills, blueberry patches, farms, and trees. Buildings were the exception now rather than the rule, scattered here and there like kids' blocks on a rug. Very different from San Diego. Very different.

"Look. There's the post office," his mother commented as they drove through Shady Point on a narrow, tree-lined street. "It's the oldest building in town."

Sanders read the sign on the brick building. "Shady Point Post Office—Established 1890." He'd been here last summer with his mother and father. And before that, too. Still, the number of days he'd spent here in his life wasn't much. Far less in total than the number of days between now and the date on his return ticket. To him, this was a distant faraway land—like Mars. Looking around, he asked, "Will Dad come and visit me here?"

"No, Sanders. I don't think he'll be traveling across the country this summer. But he'll call. I know he'll call. And I will, too. We can talk every week." She bit her bottom lip.

Sanders turned and looked out the window again. The sky was gray.

"I know this is not easy for you," his mother went on to say. "It's not easy for any of us. But you'll have more fun up here than you expect. Just look how beautiful it is. Look at all the trees!"

Sanders *was* looking at the trees. There must have been a million of them. He guessed kids in Shady Point got good at climbing.

"This was a wonderful place to grow up, you know. It will be a wonderful place for you to spend the summer, too."

Sanders looked at his mother and saw her brush her cheek with one hand. Was she crying?

"Do I have to stay the whole summer?" he asked. His mother had already explained about the return flight ticket. About how they'd gotten a good deal on airfare so that she could fly out with him to visit her father. And she had explained that a good deal meant no ticket changes. But he thought he would ask again, just in case.

"Sanders, you may surprise yourself by having a good time, you know."

His mother turned down a long dirt road. He remembered this road from last summer. He had driven down it with his mother and father. They had been a family, coming to Gram's funeral together. That had been sad. This was sad, too—a different kind of sad.

Sanders' mother parked in front of the old wooden house and honked three times. A tall man with longish white hair and a crooked nose strode out onto the porch and down the steps. It was Grandpa. He was wearing jeans, a T-shirt, and a baseball cap. Purple. Was the cap purple?

"Rose, I'm so glad to see you," his grandfather said as he opened the door on the driver's side. Sanders' mother stepped out and hugged her father. Was she crying again?

Sanders opened his own door and got out. He moved slowly because he didn't really want to get out. He wanted to get out and stretch, but not stay.

Now the hug had ended. His mother and grandfather were standing and looking at each other, face-to-face. They were holding hands, but they weren't saying anything.

That's what Sanders remembered most about his grandfather. Not saying much. His mother had been back to visit once since Gram had died. She had left Sanders and his dad for a week to come and help her father out. He wondered what they had talked about then. He wondered if his grandfather ever talked about anything much at all.

Sanders looked away, into the greenery that surrounded the house. He took the red rock out of his right jeans pocket and held it for just a minute. Then he moved it to the left pocket. He reached up to his cap (the tan one with the hound dog label) and moved it down so the brim hid his eyes. He didn't want to be here.

"How are you doing, young man?" his grandfather asked. He'd moved around the car and was standing beside Sanders now. "You've grown, you know."

Of course Sanders knew that he'd grown.

"Ready for a summer in the country?" Grandpa asked.

"Yes," Sanders answered. Only he wasn't.

"Come on inside. I have a pot of black-eyed pea soup on the stove. Hot soup's good after a long trip," his grandfather said. He reached for Sanders' duffel bag. "I'll show you where you'll be staying."

Grandpa walked up the steps and down a dark hall. Sanders followed, feeling like he was entering a foreign land.

His mother put candles on the table to make the meal more festive. Grandpa ladled the soup into ceramic bowls the color of the daytime sky. He served a salad that he said came from his garden and bread that he baked himself. But he didn't talk to Sanders much. Mostly, his mother talked and Grandpa nodded and said a few words now and then. Mom talked about what it had been like when she was a little girl. She laughed and told stories about things she had done with Gram and Grandpa.

His soup done, Sanders got up and wandered through the house. He walked into his grandfather's study and stopped to look at a picture on the wall. It was a photo of his grandparents when they were young. He'd seen it before but had never really looked at it. His grandmother had pretty eyes and a soft smile. The same pretty eyes and soft smile he remembered her having as an old woman.

There were more pictures on the desk. There was one of his mother and father, too, taken when they were much younger. It was probably from before he was born. He went over to the desk for a closer look.

No, he was in the photo. It was when he was a tiny baby. His mother was holding him in her arms. Then he noticed a picture of himself that had been underneath. This one wasn't from a long time ago. It was a recent picture his father had taken right after Sanders' last birthday. He was wearing his plaid shirt with the one purple stripe and his hound dog cap.

From down the hall Sanders heard his grandfather's

low voice. He moved to the door, straining to hear.

"It's so good to see you, Rose. I wish it wasn't so long between visits. It's been hard."

"You could have come to California for a while after Mother died, Dad. You could have come and stayed with us."

"I don't like cities much—you know that. Besides, this was the home your mother and I made together. I didn't want to leave, even for a visit. I really miss her."

"I do too, Dad."

"I'm sorry you and Buddy are having troubles. It's so important to have someone in your life you care about. Do you think you can work it out?"

Sanders put his hands over his ears. He wanted the answer to be yes, but he didn't want to take a chance at hearing no.

MARS JOURNAL NUMBER 5
Earth Date: July 1, 8:12:48 P.M.

Once every 780 days, Earth and Mars are on the same side of the sun. On that day, they're only 35 million miles apart. That's closer than usual. That's the day we Martians like to travel between the two planets. We put on our invisible space suits and our supersonic power skates, and we leap from the top of our tallest volcano, Olympus. We fly through space at the speed of light until we land on Earth. And usually,

we Martians, we land somewhere like San Diego.
That's where I landed.

I don't remember that day because it was when I
was really, really, really little. A little Martian. Now I'm a
bigger Martian. Well, a medium Martian. Except that I
look like a medium Earthling. Everyone thinks I'm a
medium Earthling. But I'm a Martian. I came here
when I was very small. Like in the picture where my
mother (my Earth mother) has long hair down past her
shoulders and is wearing a flowered hat. She's holding
a little baby and smiling. And my Earth dad is standing
next to her, wearing a purple shirt. My favorite color.
The Martian royal color. He's standing next to her with
his arm around her. And he's smiling, too. They're all
smiling—even the little baby. The little Martian baby.

MARS JOURNAL NUMBER 6
July 5, 11:31:29 A.M.

Today my mom (Earth mom) went back to San
Diego. She drove off and left me here in Shady Point.
A Martian alien in Maine. I don't know if Shady Point
has any other intergalactic travelers. It might be hard
to make friends because of being the only Martian
and all.

I wish I could leap back to San Diego with my
supersonic skates and my invisible space suit. Just fly
across the sky the way I did from the Olympus volcano

on Mars to Earth in the first place. Only I don't quite remember how I did that, since I was a baby and all. I'm not quite sure how to get back to Mars. Or even to San Diego. So I guess for now, all I can do is report back to Mars about what it's like on Earth for a kid whose parents are separating. Separating for the summer. At least I hope only for the summer.

Now, Martians, we don't like parents to separate for longer. We like parents to stay together as twos. That's why we have two moons. They keep each other company, and they remind parents to stay together. They remind parents to keep their kids with them instead of sending them away for the summer. Martian parents don't send their kids to places like Shady Point. They don't send them to places where they don't know how to leap home with their supersonic skates. Really, kids should stay with their parents. I told my Earth parents that. But they didn't understand.

9

Foreign Territory

When he woke up, Sanders didn't know where he was. He had forgotten for a moment. Then he remembered where he was and that he didn't want to be there. He didn't know what time it was because there was no clock in the room. It couldn't be too early, though. Light was seeping around the edges of the dark curtains.

Sanders wasn't sure if he should stay in bed or get up. He didn't feel at home. The sounds outside were different than the sounds at home. No city sounds like cars roaring by and garbage cans clanging. Instead he heard the rustling of leaves and the chatter of birds.

The inside sounds were different, too. Now he heard footsteps treading down the hall. Sanders sat up in bed, reached for his glasses, and put them on. He grabbed his light-up watch and checked the time. It was 8:47 (and 20 seconds). He'd slept later than usual.

He pulled the plaid comforter back and stepped out onto the cool hardwood floor. A spider ran across the room. A wolf spider? he wondered. He followed the spider's path. It scurried quickly under the closet door before he could get a closer look.

41

Sanders put his robe on, unsure about what to do next. The floor creaked as he walked across it. A sad creak, he thought. He hadn't been there for a full week yet and already he was homesick. Or had he been homesick before he even left home? Had it started when his parents first told him that things were changing? Or just when his mother left Shady Point?

He picked up the picture of his mom and dad that he had secretly taken from Grandpa's study. Borrowed, he thought—like Joey's rock. Not taken.

There was a knock. "You up?" his grandfather called through the door. "You want to come out and have some breakfast?"

Sanders tucked the photo in a drawer along with the rock and opened the door. His grandfather was dressed, once again wearing jeans, a T-shirt, and a cap. Same old jeans he'd worn every day, as far as Sanders could tell. Different T-shirt. Different color cap.

"How many of those caps do you have?" was all the good morning Sanders offered.

"Oh, a couple dozen or so," his grandfather answered, seemingly unmoved by the prickliness in Sanders' voice. Or perhaps he was unaware of it. "I collect them. Fair, dog show, baseball game, wherever I go, I get one. Then, when I get dressed, I pick the one that fits my mood. Always wear one. Always have. You want to wear any one of 'em, you can."

Sanders didn't think he did. He liked his own cap with the hound dog logo.

Grandpa looked down at Sanders' bare feet. "You bring slippers? Your feet will get cold in the mornings if you don't have some."

"No," Sanders answered. It was the first morning he hadn't gotten dressed before stepping out the door.

"Hmmm . . . Let me get you some wool socks. They'll do."

Sanders just stood there. When Grandpa brought the socks back—thick white ones with two dark blue stripes at the top—he put them on. First the left foot, then the right.

His grandfather waited. Then he asked again, "You ready for breakfast?"

"I guess," said Sanders with a shrug. He *was* hungry. Maybe you got hungry quicker in the country. Or maybe being lonely made you hungrier.

"Come on out, then, and have some cereal with me. Nothing fancy like yesterday morning. Maybe we can cook something special later on. Do you like Wheat Puffs? Or maybe Toasty Oats?"

"Toasty Oats. I like those," Sanders said. "I like them with bananas. Do you have bananas?"

"I always have bananas," Grandpa said.

It was the fifth Shady Point breakfast. But it was the first one he and his grandfather were having alone. And it was a quiet breakfast. Neither he nor his grandfather had much to say to one another. His mother had done most of the talking the last few days.

The fourth Shady Point breakfast had been pancakes with fresh strawberries from the garden. His mother had made them before she left for home. Before the last good-bye. How many good-byes was a kid supposed to say in one week?

He'd hugged her extra long when she got ready to leave. "I'll see you soon," she'd said, kissing his forehead and turning quickly so he wouldn't see her tears. He'd held his in all through the last good-bye. Then he'd stood watching her drive down the dirt road, away, still not crying. "Bye," he had whispered. "Good-bye."

"Well, how long you going to stand there, young man?" his grandfather had asked after a long while. "There's more to see here than just the tail end of a road, you know."

Sanders didn't know.

10
Looking Around

Sanders had done a lot of looking around on his own the first few days in Shady Point. His mother and grandfather had sat together inside or on the porch while Sanders explored all alone. The three of them would gather for breakfast, for lunch, and then again for dinner—all of which his mother prepared.

In between meals, Sanders walked around outside, not going much of anywhere. Just walking around outside the house, not going into town or anywhere. Just scouting.

He'd been to Shady Point before, of course. But the last summer—the summer of the funeral—hadn't been any kind of exploring trip. Sanders and his father hadn't stayed long, not even three full days. Only his mother had stayed longer.

The summer before that his grandmother had still been well. But Sanders hadn't visited Shady Point that year. No one in his family had. Instead, Gram had made a special trip out to San Diego, without Grandpa. Sanders had taken her to the zoo while she was there. (Or had she taken him?)

In fact, Sanders' last trip to Maine other than the funeral had been three years ago. And any boy can tell you three years is a very long time. Things change. Or you don't remember them. Or you didn't notice them in the first place because you were so young.

So now Mom was gone and it was just Sanders and his grandfather. They had Toasty Oats and bananas on their first day alone. That was OK, Sanders guessed. Only he figured they had already pretty much said everything they had to say to each other. And there were still 57 days to go. He'd explored just about everywhere there was to explore during the first four days. He didn't guess there was much more to see, even though his grandfather had said there was more here than just the tail end of a road. Like what? Sanders wondered, but he didn't ask.

He already knew there were no empty lots halfway between best friends' houses. No solar systems dangling above the kitchen table. No understanding cats always ready to give good advice. No mother. No father. No private tent in his own bedroom. No San Diego. Only a grandfather he didn't have all that much to say to. And maybe some snails in the garden—alien snails, of course.

Still, Sanders went along when Grandpa wanted to show him what *was* around. His grandfather had shown him the garden with the lettuce and tomatoes and all the other fresh vegetables. He'd shown him the fence he'd built, the one that needed fixing. He'd shown him the tall tree beside the house and told him just how tall it was and how you could figure the height of a tree by measuring its shadow. All these things, Grandpa had shown him. But it was all done with only a few words exchanged between the two men, grandfather and grandson. Both had things to be quiet about . . . things to keep in . . . things to keep from each other. And Sanders didn't care all that much about anything his grandfather showed him, anyway.

Mostly what Sanders wanted to do was find a private place. A place to be alone. He wanted a tent-office kind of place like he had at home. But he didn't want to ask where he could find or make this private place because then it wouldn't be private. And, although there was an extra blanket on his bed, he didn't feel like he could just up and use it to make a tent office in the middle of his room here.

However, even without his own private place, Sanders had lots of time alone. His grandfather seemed to see that he needed that time. Or maybe it was *Grandpa* who wanted to be alone. Whatever the reason, at some point every morning after breakfast, Grandpa would announce that he had "personal business" to attend to and go off somewhere on his own—into his den or outside. Meanwhile, Sanders would survey the yard one more time, search his room for the wolf spider he'd seen that one morning, write in his summer journal . . .

It felt like it had been a hundred years ago that he had left San Diego.

But this morning something different happened after breakfast. "I'd like to take you into town this afternoon," Grandpa said. "There are some things to see in this town. Did you know the post office was built more than 100 years ago?"

Sanders nodded. "Yeah," he answered. "That was a long time ago."

MARS JOURNAL NUMBER 7
Earth Date: July 8, 10:22:22 A.M.

Sometimes when you travel through space you have to go a really, really long way from home, even if the planets are all lined up in a row. Like if you travel from Mars to Earth, well, that's only 48,546,000 miles. But if you travel from Mars to Saturn, that's 743,442,000 miles. And if you want to go from Mars to Pluto, that's another 3,516,702,000 miles. And if your mother's on one planet, and your father's on another, and your best friend's somewhere else . . . Do you have any idea how far away you feel from everyone?

11

Downtown Shady Point

There were seven hellos on their trip into Shady Point. Seven—Sanders counted them. And every single one had some kind of "Haven't seen you around much lately" attached to it.

The first hello was from a short, dark kid named Eric Marnell, who lived next door to Grandpa. Sanders had noticed him tossing a ball in the neighboring yard the day before and had asked his grandfather who he was.

"Hey, Mr. Roberts!" Eric shouted as he passed them on the road. He was running fast, pulled along by a husky-like dog on a leash. "Slow down, Tammer!" he shouted, but the dog kept on going. Still, Eric managed to gasp out a sentence or two.

"Haven't seen you lately. That your grandson?"

"Yes. Eric. Sanders." It was a quick introduction because the dog was dragging its owner farther down the road.

"He's trying to train the dog," Grandpa explained after Eric had been pulled away.

"He's not doing a very good job, is he?" Sanders asked.

"No, he's not. But some things take time."

The walk to town took time, too—33 minutes and 11 seconds. Sanders hadn't meant to time, it, but he'd looked at his watch right after they said hello to Eric. Then he'd kicked a rock that just happened to be on the dirt path in front of him. A craggy gray rock with silvery slivers that had caught his eye. He kicked it first just because he wanted to kick something. He wanted to kick Shady Point, really. But the rock was as close to that as he could come. So he kicked it again and again.

"You going to kick that rock all the way to town?" his grandfather asked.

"Yeah," Sanders answered shortly. Actually, he thought Grandpa had a good idea. Sanders could have one rock in his pocket and another on the road. A good rock (the one in his pocket) and a bad rock (the one on the road). And he also thought it might be a good idea to know how long he kept the rock moving along. So he'd looked at his watch just before the first kick and again just after the last one. Thirty-three minutes and 11 seconds from the first hello (Eric's) to the last (outside the Shady Point Post Office—established in 1890).

Sanders left the rock outside the post office when they went in to look around. Grandpa wanted him to see the mural of Pilgrims coming to a new land, a new life. And he wanted to buy stamps.

"Jeb, good to see you in town again!" said the plump, gray-haired woman at the counter. "Sure don't see you around much anymore. Is this your grandson? The one we used to hear so much about?"

"It is," Grandpa answered. "Dorothy, I'd like you to meet my grandson, Rose's boy, Sanders Parker. Sanders A. Parker. Sanders, this is Mrs. Samuels. She's lived in Shady Point almost as long as I have."

"Hello," Sanders said, his hands in his pockets.

"He looks a lot like you," Mrs. Samuels said. "Except for the hair. It's been a long while since your hair was that color."

"That it has," Grandpa said. "A long while."

"He's kind of quiet like you, too, isn't he?" she asked.

"Maybe," was the whole of his grandfather's answer.

"But you know," Mrs. Samuels went on, cupping her chin in one hand and squinting, "I think he has Margaret's eyes."

His grandfather looked at Sanders intently, nodded once, and then looked away.

"So what can I do you for today, Jeb?" Mrs. Samuels asked.

"Commemoratives," he answered. "Do you have any commemoratives?"

"Just these right now," she said, pulling out three sheets of stamps and laying them on the counter. The first sheet showed African animals. The second had famous cowboys. And the third showed stars and nebulae.

"These," Sanders said, suddenly interested in the business at hand. His finger touched the Orion nebula.

His grandfather placed a ten-dollar bill on the counter and traded it for stars plus change. Then he took the sheet of star stamps and folded it up and tucked it in his shirt pocket. They said good-bye and nice to meet you and went back outside into the bright blue day.

Once out the door, Sanders retrieved his kicking rock—the gray one with the silver glint. He thought about what the lady at the post office had said. He didn't think he was like his grandfather at all. He dropped the kicking rock of Shady Point, Maine, into his pocket—next to the Mars rock from San Diego, California.

"You interested in astronomy?" his grandfather asked.

"Well, we learned about outer space in school this year," Sanders offered.

"Your grandmother liked to look at the stars at night, you know. I bought her a little handheld telescope for her 60th birthday."

Sanders hadn't known that. He knew Gram had liked

flowers and animals and making jam. He didn't know she had liked looking at stars through a telescope. He never would have guessed. "Do you still have the telescope?" he asked.

"I do," his grandfather answered.

"Do you ever use it?"

"I don't. No. Not really," Grandpa said. "I keep it right up top on the bookshelf in my den. It's a pretty little telescope. But I don't use it. No."

"Could I use it?" Sanders asked.

"Don't know about that." His grandfather explained no further.

"Do you miss her very much? Gram, I mean." Sanders asked now. Suddenly he wondered about this more than he had even the summer before, when she had died.

"Yes, I surely do," the old man said. "I surely do."

12

Hmmm . . .

They went back to town the next day. Grandpa insisted that small towns had as much or more to see in them as big cities if you just knew where and how to look. They visited the library, the Penguin Cafe, and the Nathan Hugg Dirt Museum. Finally, they stopped at the Double Dip Ice Cream Parlor where they each had a two-scoop cone. Sanders had chocolate chip and peanut supreme. His grandfather had peach melba and vanilla bean. They sat at a little round table with a red-checkered plastic tablecloth and watched the people walking along Laurel Avenue. So, yes, Sanders thought, there is stuff to see here. But he still didn't like the place.

"Can I call my dad tonight?" Sanders asked.

"Yes, of course," his grandfather answered. "I have his new number."

After they finished the ice cream, they walked quietly most of the way home. This time, Sanders had only the Mars rock in his pocket, not the Shady Point one. And this time, he didn't kick any rocks—or time the walk—or count the steps—or walk backward. He just walked quietly beside his grandfather.

That evening, Sanders talked to his father for what seemed like a long time. His father asked a lot of questions. How was he? How was his grandfather? What did he do today? What was the weather like? Had he seen any interesting insects? Climbed any trees? Met any kids? What did he think of his grandfather's garden? His grandfather's cooking? Did he get a summer library card?

Sanders answered all these questions. But he only had two of his own to ask: "Are you going to come home?" and "Can't you fix this?" Both his questions had to do with the word *separation.*

The answers his father gave made some sense. But neither was the answer Sanders had wanted to hear. Neither was the answer he had *hoped* to hear. The simple answer . . . the one-word answer . . . the "yes" answer.

Oh, his father said he missed him and that he loved him. He even told Sanders that he had taken the solar system mobile off the kitchen light fixture and put it up in his apartment. That it reminded him of his son. But he didn't say that he was coming home soon, or that Sanders could come home soon, either.

"I love you, Sanders."

"I love you, too, Dad."

"Good-bye, son."

"Good-bye."

Sanders put the phone down and walked quietly back to the room his grandfather had loaned him for the summer.

MARS JOURNAL NUMBER 8
July 10, 7:14:27 P.M.

The days on Mars are 41 minutes longer than the days on Earth. These extra minutes are Martian minutes that kids spend with their parents. Every single day of every single year. On Mars, there are always those extra 41 minutes for kids and parents to be together. No matter what. Always and forever.

Here on Earth, things take time. And you don't always have that extra time, those extra 41 minutes to take care of things just when you want to. You have to wait. Because some things take time, and you don't have it. But on Mars you do have extra time—41 minutes every day. And an extra 122 days every year. So parents can never say, "We have to wait and see, because things take time."

"Sanders?" His grandfather knocked on the door.

Sanders closed the journal and reached for the red rock—the Mars rock. He didn't answer.

"Sanders, can I come in?" his grandfather turned the knob and then pushed the door open a crack.

Sanders bit his lip and turned away. His grandfather came inside and sat next to him. Not exactly next to him—not so close as to put his arm around him. But close enough to see the tears waiting in the corners of Sanders' eyes.

"Sad call?" he asked.

"I don't want him to leave. I miss them. I miss Joey."

"Hmmm," his grandfather said, shaking his head in agreement. He didn't say, "Everything's going to be OK" or "Summer will be over before you know it" or "Don't be sad" or any number of other things. He just said, "Hmmm." But it was the kind of "Hmmm" that had more than just an "h" and a bunch of "m"s in it. It was a "hmmm" that had all kinds of other secret meanings. Most of which was, simply, "I know how you feel."

It was that "Hmmm" that made Sanders crumple. "I want to go home, Grandpa. I want *Dad* to come home. I had a whole summer planned with Joey. I miss Mom. Why couldn't I stay there? Why couldn't he stay there? Why did everything have to change?"

"Good-byes are hard. I'll grant you that, Sanders."

Sanders was rolling the red rock around and around in his hand.

"Is that the rock you kicked to the post office?"

"No," Sanders said, holding it steady now.

"A red rock? Can I take a look?"

"Yeah," Sanders said, handing over the lucky rock. Which hadn't really been lucky yet.

His grandfather took the rock and turned it over. He examined it, then closed his big square hand around it. "Nice rock," he said.

"Mars," Sanders said without even thinking. It was as if he were so filled up with everything that he just couldn't keep it all inside anymore.

"Mars?" his grandfather repeated.

Sanders didn't tell about his secret mission or how he took the rock or why he took it. He only asked, "Do you ever feel like you're really from another planet?"

Grandfather looked at him knowingly. "Yes, often I do. In fact, it seems like lately I'm clumping around on a strange planet most days. A lot of people have felt like that now and again."

He didn't press Sanders. He didn't ask to explain himself or push him to tell what was on his mind. And Sanders didn't say anymore about it. They just sat there together. Quiet.

After a time, Grandpa said, "You know, I believe you can see the planet Mars in the sky from here."

"You can?" Sanders asked.

"Yes. Especially with Gram's telescope."

13

Stargazing

They brought the flashlight and Gram's telescope. The flashlight was extra long and thick—a utility light. It was almost as long as the telescope. But the telescope was thinner and more delicate. It was made of shiny brass and had leather trim and one ring of purple at the eyepiece end. "That was Gram's favorite color," Grandpa said. "So I had it added special."

His grandfather carried the telescope. Sanders held the flashlight, beaming it ahead of them to make a path. They needed the light to guide them because it was very dark at night in Shady Point. Darker than in San Diego. There weren't streetlights along every road like there were at home. The only streetlights in Shady Point were downtown. The only night-lights were the stars.

And there were lots of stars. Many more than in San Diego, it seemed. But Grandpa said there were the same number of stars; it was just that you could see more of them here. "Some things you can see better when you get away from the city," his grandfather said. Sanders thought that maybe Grandpa was talking about more than the night sky. But he wasn't sure, and he didn't ask.

They had two other things with them. One was Gram's star chart. She had always kept it tucked in the bookshelf, Grandpa had said. So she could pull it out every now and again and read it like a book. Grandpa had left it there, tucked away and waiting for a whole year.

They had also brought along Sanders' compass—the one he carried on his keychain with the glowdog and the shiny new key. The new key to the house where he had lived with his mother and father all his life before he realized he was from Mars. The house he would go back to at the end of the summer, not knowing if his father would be back, too. Sanders knew the compass would help them locate the stars in the sky. It would help them locate Mars, too. His secret, intergalactic, true home.

So now they walked along the dirt path, not going toward town, where they had been earlier. They went in the other direction, away from town. They walked over a little hill, past the private graveyard where his grandmother was buried. They went on until they reached an open space just beyond the graveyard.

Sanders remembered standing between his mother and father in that little cemetery. His grandfather had seemed taller then, only a year before. He'd had tears running down his cheeks, Sanders remembered. It was the first time he'd seen a grown man cry. And he remembered that he had been sad himself, about Gram dying. But this year he was beginning to understand what sad was about even more than he had then.

At last they stopped. "This is a good place," Grandpa said. And it was. The sky opened up here. It was as if someone had poured a whole pitcherful of sparkly stars into a big pot of black soup. A big wide pot like the kind his grandfather used to make black-eyed pea soup. Or fresh-grown tomato soup or carrot-and-yam soup or any of the other kinds that Sanders knew Grandpa liked to make. He knew because Grandpa had told him so. He had told him that he liked to cook, especially soup.

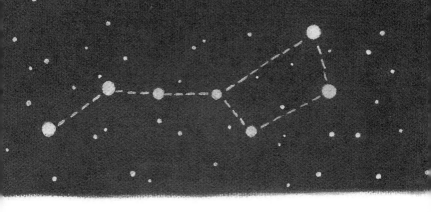

So they looked up at the star soup together. It wasn't as if they were friends. It was more as if they were working partners. Like they had a job to do together. Like he and Joey had been in the beginning before they were friends.

At first they just looked up and didn't try to figure out what any of the stars were. But Sanders realized that he knew some of the constellations—the same ones that lit the sky over his home in California, but in slightly different places. He knew some of them by name because he had learned them during the year in Mrs. Ryan's Exploration of Space unit.

"There's the Big Dipper," Sanders said, pointing it out to his grandfather. He went on to explain how it was part of Ursa Major, the Great Bear. And right below that was Boötes, the herdsman who was always chasing the bear. And how the hunter looked like an ice-cream cone.

"What kind of ice-cream cone?" Grandpa asked. "Chocolate chip, peanut supreme, or vanilla bean?"

"Chocolate chip," Sanders said. He laughed, and so did his grandfather. Suddenly Sanders realized that it was the first time he had really laughed in Shady Point.

And the first time he had heard his grandfather laugh, too.

"Shine the flashlight on the star chart, will you?" asked Grandpa. So Sanders did and his grandfather studied the chart for a moment.

"Your grandmother showed me how to read these charts," Grandpa said. "How to find the planets." And then he showed Sanders how if you followed the arc of the handle of the Big Dipper to the bottom of the ice-cream cone, the star Arcturus, and you kept following that same line down a little lower in the sky, then you would see the planet Mars. The red planet.

Sanders' eyes lifted from the star chart to the stars themselves. They followed Grandpa's finger as it traced the path from the Big Dipper to Mars. And then they both could see Mars, without the telescope. With their naked eyes.

Then his grandfather handed Sanders the telescope— his grandmother's telescope. Sanders used it to get a better look at Mars. But a minute later, Grandpa said, "That's enough, boy. Let me have the telescope again."

Sanders handed it to him. Then, with Sanders holding the flashlight and Grandpa cradling the shiny brass telescope, they walked back to the house.

MARS JOURNAL NUMBER 9
July 11, 10:20:11 A.M.

Last night I saw Mars.

MARS JOURNAL NUMBER 10
July 16, 10:20:11 P.M.

We've gone out every night this week. I always look at my home planet. At Mars. I don't tell Grandpa that I'm from Mars or that I'm a Martian. This is still a secret mission. No one knows. But Grandpa knows about the rock—at least he knows that I call it a Mars rock. Everything else is still secret. My mission. That I am only visiting Earth from 48,546,000 miles away. Because I know that on my planet—on Mars—parents stay together. So Earth can't be my planet because my parents are not together. They're having troubles. And I'm having troubles, too, because they sent me away for the whole summer. So I'm not with my mom. And I'm not with my dad. And I'm not with my best friend Joey. My Mars partner. Those are my troubles.

My mission: to change everything. I haven't figured out how to do that yet. But every night I go out with Grandpa and we find Mars in the sky. We usually go a little after sunset. That's the best time to see the planets. We've seen all the naked-eye planets. Those are the ones you can see without a telescope: Mercury, Venus, Mars, Jupiter, and Saturn. The easiest to see are Mars, Jupiter, and Venus. Mercury is a little harder to find. We look for a long time with our naked eyes. Grandpa says it's good to be able to see things with your own eyes. He holds Gram's telescope, the one he gave her for her 60th birthday. After a while, he hands it to me, and I find the planets right away. I look at them; then I give the telescope back and look with my naked eyes again.

When I talk to Dad, I tell him which planets Grandpa and I see. That way, when he looks at the model of the solar system that Joey and I made, he'll know.

14

The Treehouse

"**H**i! Aren't you Mr. Roberts' grandson?"

Eric ran alongside the falling-down fence that separated his yard from Sanders' grandfather's property. His straight black hair flopped against his forehead. Tammer, his dog, was close behind, barking and jumping up and down.

"Yeah," Sanders said. He shifted the large brown paper bag he carried from one hand to the other.

"Remember, we met last week? I was walking my dog?" Eric brushed the hair off his forehead with one hand.

"Yeah, I remember. But wasn't the dog walking *you?*" Sanders asked without stopping.

"Well, maybe," Eric answered. "I'm training him. He hasn't got it down exactly yet. But he's smart, so he'll learn. Watch this."

Sanders stopped and Eric called Tammer to his side. He commanded the dog to sit, to lie down, and even to crawl. Tammer followed these orders, but instead of sitting quietly afterward, waiting for the next command, he jumped around and wagged his tail proudly.

When the performance ended, Sanders asked, "What kind of dog is he?"

"He's part husky and part Lab. Two years old," Eric said.

"Do you think you can teach him to walk on a leash, too?"

"Maybe," Eric said. Then he asked, "What do you have in the bag?"

"Snails," Sanders answered matter-of-factly. He started to walk again.

"Snails?" Eric asked, his face lighting with interest. He leaned over the fence to see.

Sanders opened the bag, still walking along on his side. Eric walked on the other, arm trailing along the top rail, leaning toward Sanders and peering inside. "What are you going to do with them?" he asked.

"Relocate 'em," Sanders answered.

"Huh? Why?"

"I took them out of my grandpa's vegetable garden. They were eating the lettuce. I'm taking them away, to some place where they can't eat the vegetables. I figured I'd put them out back."

"Under the old treehouse?" Eric asked.

"What treehouse?" Sanders asked. Suddenly he remembered hearing his mom tell stories about a treehouse she had as a kid. But his grandfather hadn't mentioned it, and Sanders hadn't seen one.

"You don't know about the treehouse? Didn't your grandpa ever tell you about it? It was built a real long time ago. I think he built it. Sometimes I sneak up there and goof around. Want me to show you?"

"Yeah," Sanders said, "I do."

Eric climbed over the fence and Tammer squeezed under it. Together, boys and dog walked to the very back edge of the property. The treehouse was there. The tree that supported it wasn't the biggest or tallest, but it was good-sized. The remnants of the treehouse were in the lowest branches, but even these were a good distance from the ground. A rough ladder had obviously been nailed onto the front of the tree long ago. It was old and rotted and sported missing rungs. So now you'd have to hug the tree trunk to get up to the treehouse.

Sanders deposited the snails in their new home at the base of the tree. Then he followed Eric up the trunk while Tammer stood guard below. Two kids could easily fit inside the treehouse, and did.

Sanders looked around. The floorboards were rotten in places, offering glimpses of the ground below. And some of the support beams were loose. Still, there he was, sitting in an almost-private sky place.

"You're staying with your grandpa for the whole summer, aren't you?" Eric asked. Without waiting for an answer, he continued. "So what else do you do here besides relocate snails?"

Sanders answered the first question. "Yeah, the whole summer." It felt good to be talking to somebody his age. Or close to his age—Eric might be a year younger. "I wanted to stay in San Diego. My best friend's there. But my parents wanted me to come and stay with my grandpa."

"Yeah. I guess he could use some company. He mostly stays inside since your grandma died. I used to help him sometimes before. I even helped him fix that old fence some. But he stopped working on it. So what do you do besides move snails around?" Eric asked again.

"Well, one thing we've been doing is coming out at night with a telescope to look at the planets."

"You have a telescope?" Eric asked. "Boy, I'd like to see that!"

"My grandmother had one. But you can see some of the planets without a telescope, even. Like Mars. The naked-eye planets they're called. The ones you can see without a telescope."

"Which ones besides Mars?" Eric asked.

"Mercury, Venus, Jupiter, Saturn. And Mars. Those are the naked-eye planets."

"You come out every night?"

"Well, we have this week."

"You know, I used to see your grandpa around a lot before your grandma died. He used to fix things for everybody in town. All the time. But he doesn't do all that much fixing anymore. My mom says he's changed since his wife died. I liked her, your grandma. She was really nice. So he really likes to come out at night and look at naked planets?"

"Yeah, he does. I do, too," Sanders said.

"But you have a telescope? I mean your grandma did. Do you use it? Could I see it?"

"I don't know," said Sanders. "Grandpa is pretty careful with that telescope. I think it reminds him of Gram. He doesn't even let me hold it for long."

Their conversation turned to other things. And then they spent some time just being quiet and looking out over the wooded ground. Sanders wasn't sure how long they spent in the tree, but it wasn't that long. Only long enough to see that it was a good place to be and that tree climbing had its virtues. Long enough to see that empty city lots had a certain something missing. Long enough to wonder if this had been the treehouse his mother had played in.

It could probably be fixed, thought Sanders. Then it could be my private summer place. My private summer place where once in a while I could have company. And maybe even bring Gram's telescope up here and look at the stars with a friend.

After they climbed down and said good-bye, Sanders went in search of his grandfather. He was probably in his study, looking through his desk things and seeing to his "personal business," as he did most mornings. Or at least that's what he always said he was doing.

But Sanders didn't find his grandfather in the study. He knew Grandpa wouldn't go far from the house without telling Sanders his whereabouts. Even if they didn't talk all that much, Grandpa wouldn't go away without saying so. So if he looked around close by, Sanders figured, he'd find him.

Which he did—just over the little hill that was beyond the house. The hill they traveled over every night, carrying the flashlight and Gram's telescope. The hill that overlooked the small private cemetery where Sanders had stood the year before beside his mother and father.

Sanders came up behind his grandfather slowly and quietly. The old man was sitting on a small stone bench, facing the plot where his wife was buried. His head was down and he was talking softly. Sanders heard some of his whispered words. ". . . becoming a fine young man. Our Rose's son . . . You were right . . . wonderful grandson . . . thank our lucky stars."

Sanders backed away. This was private time. He walked back to the house to wait for Grandpa to finish his "personal business" and return.

15

Pretending

Sanders was sitting on the porch whittling when his grandfather returned. He was using his grandfather's pocketknife to do the carving. Grandpa had loaned it to him for the summer, after showing him how to use it. He'd taught Sanders how to hold the knife properly, how to shave a thin sheet off a piece of wood, and then begin carving a shape. Sanders was trying to make a rocket ship. He thought he might like to send it to Joey. But what he was ending up with was a toothpick and a whole lot of wood shavings. He didn't want to send a toothpick to Joey.

"Nice work," his grandfather said when Sanders held up the whittled-down stick. "We need some more sticks around here." Then he sat down next to Sanders on the porch swing. "Don't have enough," he added, smiling just a little.

"I wanted to make something else," Sanders said. "But I'm just not very good at whittling."

"You'll get better. Takes time," his grandfather replied.

Sanders kept whittling. As he worked, he told his grandfather about meeting Eric. And about seeing the treehouse and climbing up into it.

"You know, I built that treehouse for your mother more than 30 years ago," Grandpa said. "That's a long time. I'm not sure it's too safe after all these years."

"Did she help you?" Sanders asked. He wondered if his mother had liked helping her father as much as Sanders liked helping his. If she'd felt as proud as he did. He wondered if she'd figured her father could fix anything just like he'd always figured his father could. Until this summer, when his mother and father said they had problems and his father couldn't seem to fix them as easily as he could a broken lock. He wondered if she missed her father as much as he missed his.

"Oh yes. Yes, she helped me," his grandfather answered. "She was a good little helper. Good with a hammer, your mother. She liked to build things with me. But more than that, she liked to help her mother. They were very close."

"Grandpa . . . I saw you," Sanders whispered.

"Yes? Did you?" he cocked his head and looked sideways at Sanders.

"Yes," Sanders said. "I came to find you after I saw the treehouse. But you weren't here. So I went looking. I went over the hill and I saw you there. I heard you talking . . . "

"I see. And?"

"Were you talking to Gram?" Sanders asked.

"I like to think I was," his grandfather answered,

nodding his head. "I like to think so." His grandfather looked over at him. "I like to think she can hear me. But mostly," he went on, "even if I just pretend she can, well . . . I feel better being able to say what I'm feeling inside."

Sanders sat quietly for a minute. "Grandpa . . . I pretend stuff sometimes, too," Sanders said as he looked down.

"Do you?" his grandfather asked.

"Yes, I pretend I'm from Mars. That that's my real home. Because on Mars, parents don't get separated."

"Oh, don't they?"

"Well, that's what I pretend," Sanders said.

"Hmmm . . . " his grandfather said. "I see."

It was the same "Hmmm . . ." he'd said the other night. The one that didn't mean anything in particular but at the same time, meant everything. It meant "I know." And "I understand." And "I hear what you're saying."

"Grandpa," Sanders asked, "do you think we could fix the treehouse?"

"Yes. I think maybe we could."

MARS JOURNAL NUMBER 11
July 18, 3:02:02 P.M.

I can see Mars with my naked eyes. But I can see it better with Gram's telescope. With Gram's telescope I can see more of my home planet. I can see reddish places and greenish places and maybe even polar ice caps. And right nearby in the sky, right near Mars, I can see Spica. Spica is the 14th brightest star in the sky. It is a blue-white star. I can see the blue when I look through the telescope. From way down here on Earth, Spica and Mars look close together. I know they must be really far away from each other in space. But they look close together. They look like two friends in the sky. The red planet and the blue star. If they could share the colors they shine back to Earth, they would mix them to shine purple.

It's good to have a friend. To have somebody to share with.

MARS JOURNAL NUMBER 12
July 19, 2:01:01 P.M.

If you look in the nighttime sky you can see lots of friends. Like the constellation Boötes the herdsman. And he's always chasing Ursa Major and Ursa Minor. Those are the Great Bear and the Little Bear. He always wants to be with the two bears, so he follows them all the time. And Boötes has his dogs, too. They're in the constellation Canes Venatici. They're his companions and they help him follow those two bears. Then there's Procyon. That's another dog—the little dog star. It's always in the sky near Venus. So those two are friends. Of course, Mars has its two potato moons—two potato friends. Jupiter has 16 moons, and they keep orbiting around Jupiter together because they're all good friends. Wherever you look in the sky, you can see that friends like to be together. Just like Joey and me. And just like Eric and me. My two good friends.

16

Repair Work

They got ready to fix the treehouse early in the morning, before the sun was fully up and it got too hot. They both dressed the same: in jeans, T-shirts, and sneakers. Work clothes, the kind of clothes Grandpa wore every day.

"What about a cap?" asked Grandpa. Sanders looked over the assortment that hung from hooks by the back door. He didn't want to wear the purple one, the one Grandpa had worn the first day.

"That one!" he said, pointing to the cap that was deep blue like the midnight sky. It had a moonflower embroidered on the front—and a secret message written on the inside edge of the band. Sanders had seen the message once when his grandfather had taken the cap off and put it upside down on the kitchen table. Inside in small purple letters was written, "Thank my lucky stars." Sanders had read it and asked his grandfather why there was something written there.

"Your grandmother gave me this cap as a gift," he'd told Sanders. "She wrote the message."

So that was the cap Sanders decided to wear to work on the treehouse.

They ate breakfast quickly and quietly and then were off, heading to the back edge of the property where the tall tree stood. They also made a few trips to the shed on the side of the house, collecting supplies.

Sanders helped his grandfather carry a big piece of plywood to replace the treehouse floor. He helped him carry a tall ladder so they could climb up without hugging the tree trunk. He helped him carry the 2 x 4s that they would use to shore up the supports and cut into new rungs for the built-in ladder.

Then Sanders' grandfather put on his carpenter's apron. "Used to wear this all the time," he said, "when I fixed things. Used to help people all over town, you know. But I haven't worn it much lately."

"Don't you still fix things?" asked Sanders.

"Not like I used to," replied Grandpa slowly. "Guess I had a lot of things to fix for myself, Sanders. Things I didn't need my apron for."

Sanders wasn't exactly sure what his grandfather meant, but he didn't ask him to explain. He just watched as Grandpa filled the pockets of the apron.

"What are you putting in there?"

"These are 16-penny nails," his grandfather said as he put a handful in one pocket. "These are 20-penny nails," he said, putting a handful in another pocket. "And this is

a claw hammer," he explained.

Grandpa went on loading up his pockets, adding a pencil and a tape measure. Then he asked Sanders to carry the handsaw. They walked back to the tree, Sanders scurrying to keep up with his grandfather's long strides.

"Let's start with the rungs," Grandpa said. He showed Sanders how to use the claw hammer to pull off the ones that were rotted.

"Best to start fresh," Grandpa commented, "with new rungs. How wide do you think they should be?"

"About like this," Sanders said. He held his two hands apart to show how wide.

His grandfather measured. "Fourteen inches," he said.

"Now take the tape measure and the pencil. Mark off 14-inch strips on the boards. Then we'll cut the new rungs."

So Sanders measured and marked. Then his grandfather showed him how to hold the saw. He held the board so Sanders could cut each rung off. It was hard, and in the end, Grandpa finished the sawing. But Sanders started it.

Then his grandfather held the first rung against the trunk of the tree. Carefully avoiding his grandfather's gnarled fingers, Sanders started each nail. Then he handed the hammer to his grandfather. Sanders held the rung steady while Grandpa finished driving the nails into the tree.

They did the second rung in the same way, working together. Then they stood back to look at the two boards that climbed partway up the tree trunk.

"Hey! Hey! Hey!" Eric shouted as he came running up to them. "What's going on? What are you doing?"

"Well, young man, what does it look like we're doing?" Sanders' grandfather asked.

But before Eric could respond, Sanders explained, "We're fixing the old treehouse."

"Mr. Roberts, you're fixing things again? Can I help?" Eric asked.

Grandpa looked at Sanders, who nodded.

"Yes, you can," Grandpa answered. So now there were three of them on the job. They worked together the rest of the morning and got all the rungs up. By lunchtime, you could climb up the tree again using the built-in ladder. Sanders and Eric both climbed up easily and stood on the old, rotted floorboard.

"Good job," Eric said to Sanders. The two boys shook hands solemnly and climbed down. Sanders' grandfather was there at the base of the tree, his hands on his hips and a smile on his lips. A wide, happy-looking smile that Sanders had never seen on the old man's face before. The sight made Sanders smile, too.

"Let's go back to the house and eat," Grandpa said to the boys. "We can finish tomorrow morning."

Sanders and his grandfather walked back, side by side,

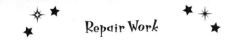

Eric zigzagging along beside them. "Do you want to eat with us?" Sanders asked Eric.

"Sure," he said. And they all went inside and ate leftover tuna casserole.

MARS JOURNAL NUMBER 13
July 20, 12 noon exactly

Some things take time. It takes 687 days for Mars to make an orbit around the sun. It takes 12 years for Jupiter to make an orbit. Saturn takes 29 years; Uranus takes 84; and Pluto, 248. Some things take time. But the time it takes some things is shorter on Earth than on other places, other planets. It only takes 365 days for Earth to orbit around the sun. A year on Mars is twice as long as a year is on Earth. A year on Pluto is 248 times longer than a year on Earth. So maybe it seems really hard to have to wait a very long time for some things here on Earth. Like waiting for a summer to be over so you can be with your best friend again. Or waiting to see your parents. But it could be an even longer wait if you were really from Mars. So you might really rather be from Earth, after all.

17
Naked Planets

"**W**e did it, Grandpa! It's fixed!"

Sanders and his grandfather stood side by side beneath the tree, proudly surveying their work. They'd finished earlier in the day but were just now walking back to take an early-evening look at the treehouse. A second look. An after-supper look.

"You might want to write to your mother and tell her you fixed her treehouse, you know," Grandpa said.

Sanders smiled. He might do that. His mother's treehouse was fixed—and he had helped to do it.

Then Grandpa shook his head. "Strange," he said. "I built this treehouse 30 years ago. Strong. It was strong. But then, after your mother grew up and moved away, it stood unused for so many years. So many years with no one paying it any attention. And look how quick it was to fix— just a few mornings of work. But it took years before I got around to it . . . "

"Some things take time, Grandpa," Sanders said.

His grandfather put an arm around Sanders' shoulders. "Yes, they do, don't they? I guess it wasn't time until now."

"Hmmm . . . " Sanders said, sounding a lot like his grandfather.

The old man laughed. "I'm going to go take care of some 'personal business' now. Is Eric going to meet you here soon?"

"Yep. I promised to show him the naked planets at sunset," Sanders said.

"Naked planets?"

"Well, naked-eye planets. He calls them the naked planets. I promised to show him Mars, Venus, and Jupiter. I think we can see those from here even at sunset. Oh, and I want to show him Procyon, the little dog star. I thought he'd like that one because of Tammer."

"And you have the flashlight in your backpack so you can get back after dark?" his grandfather asked.

"Yeah. I have the flashlight," Sanders said. He had his summer journal with him, too, but he didn't mention that.

"OK, I'll see you back at the house."

"Yeah," Sanders said, starting to climb up the rungs on the tall tree. "See you in a little bit, Grandpa."

MARS JOURNAL NUMBER 14
July 20, 7:30:00 P.M.

Sunset on Earth is a good time. I wonder what sunset is like on the other planets. I don't remember Martian sunsets. I don't remember having a grandfather on Mars. On Earth you have sunsets and grandfathers. I don't know if you do on Mars. But even a Martian can have a grandfather on Earth.

Mars is a small planet. It's not the smallest—Pluto is. But it's smaller than Earth. Kind of like Shady Point is smaller than San Diego. But Mars is a good planet, even if it is small. Like Shady Point has good things about it even if it isn't San Diego and doesn't have an empty lot that is halfway between my house and Joey Ferraro's house. Shady Point has my grandpa's vegetable garden and a nighttime sky that's so clear and bright and my mother's treehouse and the Nathan Hugg Dirt Museum and Eric Marnell and his dog, Tammer . . . and Grandpa. Who, I'm beginning to think, must be a Martian, too.

The Nathan Hugg Dirt Museum is a very good place to go. Nathan Hugg was a person who lived in Shady Point. He liked to travel—just like I do, to Mars. But he wasn't an interplanetary traveler. He just liked to travel all over the country. Everywhere he went, every single city or state, he collected a little bottle of dirt. Then he came back to Shady Point and started a museum. He put all the little bottles of dirt from all over the country on display. So now you can see how different every kind of dirt from other places looks.

I would like to start the Sanders A. Parker Interplanetary Dirt and Rock Museum. It'd have little jars of dirt and rocks from each of the planets in our solar system and even some other solar systems. But that will take a while to do. Right now I only have one interplanetary rock. The red Martian rock I took from Joey. For a long time I didn't think it was lucky. He said it was, but I didn't think so. But maybe it is. Maybe it is lucky.

My mother sends me a letter or a postcard every single day. Well, they don't come on Sundays. But she writes one every day. And I talk to my dad on the phone a lot. They each tell me they love me. They tell me they are trying to work things out. My Martian mission was to stay in San Diego so I could tell them what to do from a kid's point of view, from a Martian point of view. But maybe it's not a Martian's job to know what everybody else should do, even if they are your parents and you want them to stay together. Because everything takes time. And won't they still be my parents if they get back together or even if they don't?

"Hey, Sandy! I'm on my way up!" Eric shouted.

Sanders closed his summer journal and put it inside his backpack. "Ready," Sanders said, watching Eric climb up the rungs.

He reached back inside the backpack and felt for his grandmother's star chart. There was something crumply in the bottom of the bag, and he pulled it out to see what it was. He opened the wadded-up paper.

It was Mrs. Ryan's good-bye card. He read the words again:

Every good-bye has a hello in it. Find it.

Fondly,

Mrs. Ryan

"So show me some naked planets," Eric said breathlessly, as he arrived at the top of the ladder.

18

Spiders

Sanders had discovered that the treehouse made a good private office. Actually, it was a better private office than his tent office back home in San Diego.

Of course, he hadn't been looking for a private office space so much in the last few days. He hadn't felt any real reason to go off and be alone. Oh, he still liked quiet, alone time. But now it was a more friendly alone time. And a happier one. So that's probably why he hadn't really been looking for a private space when he suddenly realized that the treehouse had turned into the best one ever.

One reason he liked this private office better than the one in San Diego was that it could be both private and out in the world at once. He could sit by himself but, at the same time, he could see the world and the wild things going about their lives around him. In the daytime, he could see all the birds and animals (and even some bugs). And at night he could see all the stars and many of the planets (including his home planet). And if he wanted to, he could have company in his private office and not feel squished. All these were reasons why this private office was better than the one in San Diego. That one was a hiding-away kind of office that kept everything else out. This was an out-in-the-open office that put him in the middle of things.

His grandfather said if he didn't know better he'd think Sanders lived in the treehouse. But he did know better because they saw lots of each other. They had breakfast together every morning. And most evenings, they walked out in the clearing past the graveyard to stargaze. And at those times they found that they had things to say to each other. They had more to talk about than Sanders would ever have thought possible just a few weeks ago.

Pretty much each day, though, Sanders would spend some alone time in his mother's old treehouse. It pleased him to know that she had helped to build it the first time and that he had helped fix it.

He wished he could take his grandmother's telescope up in the treehouse with him. It would make it easier to see things that were far away. He had asked his grandfather, but Grandpa had said, "I'd prefer that I was with you when you use the telescope."

This morning, as he was eating breakfast, Sanders was thinking about his grandfather's words. He never actually said I couldn't use the telescope on my own, Sanders thought. Maybe if I borrow it and am real careful and bring it back safe, he'll realize he can trust me with it.

So, later that morning, he took it while his grandfather

was out in the garden. Sanders slipped the telescope into his backpack. He dropped his spider atlas in there, too. Then he left the house, calling out as he passed the garden. "Hey, Grandpa! I'm going out to the treehouse for a little while."

"OK. Have fun. See you back here for lunch."

Eric had become a regular up in the tree. Of course, he had been all along, even before Sanders knew about the treehouse. Before it was fixed. But now it was a place they shared. So it wasn't a total surprise to find Eric there waiting when Sanders climbed up the ladder.

"Hey," said Eric.

"Hey, yourself," returned Sanders. He sat down and unzipped his backpack. He reached in carefully, then hesitated and pulled out only the spider atlas. He leafed through a few pages before laying it open on the treehouse floor.

"You know," Eric said, pushing his hair off his forehead, "you never said how come your parents sent you to Shady Point for the whole summer. Don't you miss them?"

"Yeah, well," Sanders said. He hadn't talked about the whole thing out loud to anyone yet, except to his grandfather.

"How come?" Eric asked again. He'd brought two apples and a bag of chips. He opened the bag and offered some chips to Sanders, who accepted.

The spider atlas was opened to the tarantula page. Sanders traced around and around the picture of the large tarantula spider with one finger before answering.

Staring at the spider's hairy legs, he said, "They're having trouble." He still didn't completely understand what that meant, other than that it wasn't good. "They may separate," he added quickly, still not looking up. His eyes skimmed across the fun fact on the spider page: *If a tarantula is upset, it will pull hair from its abdomen and throw it at its prey.*

"Oh," Eric said knowingly. He stuffed a handful of chips into his mouth.

Sanders didn't say anything else. He turned to a page that showed the trapdoor spider. Silently he read: *Trapdoor spiders shut themselves in burrows to protect themselves from their enemies.*

"My parents are separated," Eric said matter-of-factly.

Sanders looked up from the trapdoor spider.

"They got divorced two years ago," Eric added. He reached into his paper bag and pulled out the apples. He kept one and handed the other to Sanders.

Sanders took a big bite out of the apple before asking, "Weren't you upset?"

"Yeah, I was. But it's OK now. I don't see my dad every day like I used to. But I talk to him on the phone every week. And I spend vacations with him. I know he loves me. Besides, my mom and me get along pretty good." Eric flicked his hair off his forehead again and took another bite of his apple as if he were talking about just regular old stuff.

"Can I see that book?" Eric asked. Sanders handed it to him. Eric flipped through some of the pages. He looked carefully at a picture and then read the fun fact aloud. " 'Female wolf spiders have special hairs on their bodies with knobs on the end so their young can hold on when they ride piggyback.'

"Cool!" Eric commented. "So the mom spiders really take care of their babies?" he wondered out loud.

"I guess some of them do," Sanders said. He straightened his glasses, trying to see more clearly what looked like it might be a squirrel mother with a baby squirrel in a tree hollow some 15 feet away. "My mom and I get along, too," he said. "But my parents wanted to be alone this summer while they try to figure things out."

"Right," Eric said. "Things were bad when my parents first split up, too. My mom was real sad. But it's better now."

"I guess it's hard for parents, too," Sanders said.

"Yeah, guess so. Hey, listen to this," Eric said, pointing to a picture of an orb spider. " 'Baby spiders can make perfect webs shortly after hatching.' "

Carefully, very carefully, Sanders pulled the telescope out of his backpack. He wanted to get a better look at that squirrel and her baby. He stood up and leaned over the railing with the telescope positioned over his right eye.

"You brought your grandmother's telescope! Can I see? Let me look! Let me see it!" Jumping up, Eric reached over and grabbed for the telescope.

Sanders was startled, and his fingers loosened their grip. The two boys stood staring as the telescope tumbled to the ground.

19

In Pieces

"**O**h man, I didn't mean to break it, Sanders. It was an accident. I'm really sorry."

The two boys crouched beneath the treehouse, Sanders cradling the cracked and scratched telescope, its lens broken into seven craggy pieces. Carefully, Sanders picked up each fragment and placed it inside his upside-down hound dog cap.

"I'm really sorry," Eric said again.

Sanders didn't say anything in response. He just hunkered down there, gazing at the broken pieces, the scratched and dented brass, and the purple band that had come loose.

"How much do you think a new one would cost?" Eric asked. "I've got $17.00 at home I can give you. Maybe I can get some more money from my mom."

Sanders looked up at Eric. His new friend. It wasn't Eric's fault, though he would have liked it to have been. But he knew it wasn't. He knew he'd borrowed one too many things.

"I wasn't supposed to take it," he finally said. "I borrowed it without asking. It's not your fault."

"Wow, I bet your grandpa's going to be mad. What are you going to do?"

"I don't know," Sanders said, still staring at his grandmother's telescope. "Maybe I can fix it."

"I don't think so. Not so your grandpa wouldn't know, anyway. Boy, am I sorry. You want me to tell him I bumped you? Maybe he won't be so mad. If it wasn't for me grabbing at it, you wouldn't have dropped it."

"No, I wasn't supposed to take it. I wouldn't have dropped it if I hadn't taken it," Sanders said. He folded his cap around the broken pieces to protect them. "I better go back now," he said. "My grandfather's expecting me for lunch. I don't know what I'm going to do."

"OK," Eric said, a certain amount of relief in his voice. "I'll see you later, Sandy. Good luck."

"Yeah," said Sanders.

"Have a good time?" Grandpa asked when Sanders entered the kitchen.

"It was OK," was all Sanders said. His grandfather didn't push him for more. He never pushed him to tell or talk. Though this time, Sanders kind of wished he would. Then the telling would be over and whatever was going to happen would happen. But he wasn't brave enough to start the telling all on his own. Not yet, anyway.

After lunch, Sanders didn't go back outside. He headed upstairs to his room.

"Not going back to the treehouse?" his grandfather asked in surprise.

"Not just now," Sanders answered.

"Not meeting Eric today?"

"Met him already," Sanders said.

And his grandfather didn't ask any more than that. He went about his own business while Sanders, alone in his room, discovered for sure that the telescope couldn't be fixed. At least, *he* couldn't fix it.

Some things take more than time to fix, Sanders thought. He didn't quite know what that something more was.

20

Borrowed— and Broken

They didn't go stargazing that week at all. Sanders had all kinds of excuses for not going. He said that he didn't feel like it. Or that he had other things to do. Or that he was meeting Eric in the treehouse to look at naked planets.

As usual, his grandfather didn't push him. "When you're ready," he said when Sanders once again answered his request with, "Not tonight. I don't feel like it tonight, Grandpa."

Actually, Sanders wasn't sure if he meant he didn't feel like going stargazing, or that he didn't feel like telling the truth about the telescope.

By the fifth night, Sanders was ready to tell. As ready as he would ever be, anyway. Because, more than anything, he knew he couldn't put it off any longer. But even so, he had to edge up to the telling.

That evening he went up to his room and collected

some things. He took them into the kitchen where his grandfather was sitting, drinking English breakfast tea, even though it was after dinner. As he sipped, Grandpa was turning the pages of a book of tips for tomato gardeners. Sanders sat down beside him.

"Grandpa," Sanders said as he set a picture down on the table. It was the one he had borrowed from his grandfather's study—the one where his parents were young and he was a baby and they were all happy together.

Next to the picture, he put Joey's red rock—the Mars rock. He kept the broken telescope out of sight, in his lap, bundled up in a purple T-shirt.

"Grandpa," Sanders said again.

"Yes?" his grandfather answered, looking up from the tomato tips.

"I have to tell you something. You see, I kind of borrowed some things."

"Did you?" his grandfather asked, picking up the picture of Sanders and his family. "I was wondering where this was. You borrowed it, did you?"

"Yes," Sanders said.

"Without asking?"

"I was going to give it back," Sanders said.

"Well, that *is* what borrowing means," his grandfather commented, returning the picture to the table.

When Sanders didn't say anything, his grandfather touched the rock. "Isn't this your Martian rock?" he asked.

"Yes. Only it's not really my rock. I borrowed it, too. It was Joey's rock. You remember who Joey is, right? My best friend in San Diego. He collects rocks."

"Does Joey know you borrowed it?"

"No, he doesn't."

"I see," his grandfather said. "I'm sure you thought you had a good reason for taking it. But don't you think maybe you ought to ask before you borrow other people's things?"

"Yes," Sanders said without saying anything more. He still wasn't feeling quite ready to say what he had to say. To explain what he'd done. What he wished with all his heart that he hadn't done.

Both grandson and grandfather were quiet, each thinking his own thoughts. After a time, Grandpa broke the silence. "Is there something more you want to tell me?"

"Yes," Sanders said.

His grandfather waited out the silence that followed.

Sanders took a deep breath. "I borrowed Gram's telescope," he said.

"And?"

"And I broke it," Sanders admitted. He gently placed his purple T-shirt on the table and folded it back to reveal the sad, injured telescope.

21
Figuring Things Out

The next day was quiet. Sanders knew his grandfather was angry—really angry. He knew because Grandpa hardly talked to him at breakfast. But now it wasn't like the quiet times they had shared before. Now it was an angry kind of quiet.

Toward the end of the meal, Grandpa cleared his throat. "Think it's about time to send Joey's rock back, don't you?"

"I suppose it is," Sanders said, stirring his soggy cereal with his spoon.

"I'll get you a box," Grandpa said. He went down into the basement and came back with a small, empty box. Sanders took it upstairs to his room to pack the rock inside.

Before he taped the box shut, it hit Sanders that he should put something else in it. He should send Joey the gray and silver rock he'd kicked all the way downtown to the post office. That way Joey could add a Shady Point rock to his collection. And maybe it would help to make up for not having the red Mars rock for most of the summer.

Then Sanders walked to the post office to mail the box, along with a note to Joey. His grandfather didn't come with him.

At lunchtime, Sanders tried to talk about repairing the telescope. "I'll get a job," he said. "I'll work for as long as it takes to earn enough money to fix the telescope."

"No," Grandpa said. "No. Besides, I'm not sure it *can* be fixed, Sanders. Some things can't, you know."

"Oh."

At the end of a quiet dinner, Sanders said, "Do you want me to leave early, Grandpa?"

His grandfather looked up from his pork chop and peas and said, "What?"

"I can't change my plane ticket—it would be too expensive. But I could take a bus back to San Diego."

Grandpa lowered his eyes again. "No, Sanders," he said quietly. "I don't want you to leave early."

Sanders almost wished his grandfather would yell at him. That he would tell him he was an awful grandson and he wished he had never invited him to visit. But he didn't. He was just quiet.

And because his grandfather was so quiet, Sanders didn't know what he was thinking. Nor did he ask him. He was afraid to know what the old man was thinking, Sanders realized.

The quiet continued for the next week. Every morning Sanders and his grandfather had breakfast together. Then they went off on their own.

Every noon they had lunch together. Then Sanders would go outside to meet Eric or to sit in the treehouse by himself. Grandpa would go into his study and close the door.

And every evening, they had dinner together. But they didn't go stargazing afterward—not even to look at the naked-eye planets.

Then one day, when Sanders was sitting on the bed writing a letter to his mother, there was a knock on the door. He had been telling his mother about the treehouse, but not about the telescope.

The knock was followed by a voice. "Sanders, I'd like to talk to you. Can I come in?"

"I guess," said Sanders.

His grandfather entered the room with a shopping bag in one hand. He sat down next to Sanders on the bed. "I'd like to talk to you about what happened."

"I'm so sorry, Grandpa," said Sanders all in a rush. "I won't ever borrow anything again without asking. I promise I won't."

"I know that. I believe you. But that's not what I came to say."

"Are you still mad at me?" Sanders asked.

"I was never really mad at you. Disappointed, yes. But not mad. Mad wouldn't help anything, you know."

He continued. "I've been thinking, Sanders. And I figured something out. That's what I wanted to talk to you about."

"What did you figure out?"

"I finally figured out that holding on to things doesn't bring people back, Sanders. That holding on to the good that used to be just keeps out the good that is right now. See, I loved your grandma so much. I didn't want to lose any part of her. But now I see that she left me something much more important than a telescope. She left me a grandson so much like her I can look in his eyes and see her. I figured out that your grandmother may be gone, but I still have a family. And you helped me figure that out, Sanders. So how could I be mad at you?"

Sanders couldn't answer. He didn't know what to say.

"Anyway, I have something for you, Sanders. And I want you to know it's not a loan. It's not something you have to borrow. It's a gift. It's something I know your grandmother would have wanted me to give you. So it's really a gift from both of us. Because we love you."

He reached into the shopping bag and pulled out a slender package wrapped in starry paper.

Slowly and carefully, Sanders took off the wrapping paper. Inside was a brass telescope with a purple band.

"Gram's telescope?" Sanders asked, his eyes wide with amazement. "You fixed it?"

"Not exactly," Grandpa replied. "I had to take it to someone to have a new lens put in. I couldn't do that myself. But I knocked out some of the dents and polished up the scratches as well as I could."

Sanders stared down at the telescope in his hands. There were still a few dents, he saw. And if you looked carefully, you could see where it had been scratched. He

held it up to his eye and focused it, looking out the window. It worked.

"Gram's telescope," he said with satisfaction as he lowered it.

"Better than Gram's telescope," his grandfather said. "It's *your* telescope now."

"Mine to keep?"

"Yes. I think that's what your grandma would have wanted, Sanders. There is one thing, though," the old man continued.

"What's that?"

"Well, when you leave Shady Point, I won't have a telescope here anymore. So, I'm wondering if it would be OK with you if maybe later in the year I come out to San Diego. That way I can borrow your telescope. Maybe go out looking at stars with you there. Because I'm kind of getting used to going stargazing at night, you know."

Sanders turned the telescope around in his hands. Then he noticed the engraving that had been added—*Thank my lucky stars.*

MARS JOURNAL NUMBER 15
August 8, 12:34:56 P.M.

My name is Sanders A. Parker and I am from the planet Earth. On Earth, I have a mother and a father and a grandfather and a grandmother (even if she did die) and two best friends.

You can see a lot of stars in the sky at night on the planet Earth. Sometimes you can see more of them from a town named Shady Point than you can from a city named San Diego. But there are the same number of stars no matter where you're looking from.

In the daytime, you don't see the stars at all because the sun shines so bright it hides their light. But the stars are there just the same. Like when you're not with all your family at the same time in the same place, you can't see everybody all at once. But even when they're not right there with you, where you can see them, they're still your family. They're still there. Just like the stars.